Nina's Waltz

by Corinne Demas

illustrated by Deborah Lanino

ORCHARD BOOKS   NEW YORK

Thank you to Alicia Ciccone, Courtney Hemsworth,
and their parents—D.L.

Orchard Books, A Grolier Company
95 Madison Avenue, New York, NY 10016

Manufactured in the United States of America
Printed and bound by Phoenix Color Corp.
Book design by Mina Greenstein
The text of this book is set in 14 point Galliard.
The illustrations are acrylic.

10 9 8 7 6 5 4 3 2 1

Library of Congress Cataloging-in-Publication Data
Demas, Corinne.
Nina's waltz / by Corinne Demas ; illustrated by Deborah Lanino.
p.   cm.
Summary: Nina must step in for her dad and play her special song at the fiddle
competition when he is stung by wasps.
ISBN 0-531-30281-4 (trade : alk. paper)
ISBN 0-531-33281-0 (library : alk. paper)
[1. Fathers and daughters—Fiction. 2. Violin—Fiction. 3. Songs—Fiction.
4. Contests—Fiction.] I. Lanino, Deborah, ill. II. Title.
PZ7.D39145 Ni   2000 [E]—dc21   99-54152

For my daughter, Artemis, and my cousin Alex,
two fine fiddlers—C.D.

To Heidi, Gary, and Andrew—D.L.

We left before it was quite morning.

My mother had a thermos of coffee for my father and a thermos of hot cocoa for me. My little brother, K.J., was bobbing up and down in the doorway. He wanted to come, too, but Mom said firmly, "No."

She leaned into the car window and kissed us good-bye. "Take care, you two." She patted the side of the car, the yellow sedan that's older than I am.

I turned to wave as we drove away. I knew she didn't want us to go. If Daddy stayed home for the weekend, there were some odd jobs he could do for money.

The sun was coming up just as we hit the highway. The fields were all misty with dew.

"Sleepy?" Daddy asked me.

"Not anymore," I said.

"Want to check that we've got my fiddle?" Daddy asked.

I smiled. Daddy would never forget his fiddle, but I looked in the back anyway. There was Daddy's battered fiddle case, covered with stickers from all the places he had been. My own fiddle case still looked new. I hadn't brought it along, though.

"It's fine," I said.

Daddy is the best fiddler I know. The best in the whole state. In the whole country. And Daddy was going to play his new tune, the one he wrote for me, "Nina's Waltz."

"If I win the contest," he told Mom last week, "I'll have two hundred dollars clear."

"If you win, Nick," Mom said.

"He'll win," I said.

"Your father would want to go to play even if there weren't prize money," said Mom.

Daddy gave her one of his grins. And Mom just shook her head, the same way she did when K.J. spilled paint all over the kitchen floor.

Two hawks were circling over the fields by the highway as we drove along. I could hear their high-pitched calls. I strained to watch them until they were lost in the sky.

"Want to sing a little?" Daddy asked after a while.

"Sure," I said. So we did. We sang all the way north, as the flat farmland turned to hills and the hills turned to mountains. We sang sad songs and silly songs. We sang short songs and songs that went on for miles. By the time we reached the state border, we were all sung out. Daddy pulled off the road, and we took a coffee and hot cocoa break. Then we were back on the highway again. Daddy started humming the tune he was going to play at the fiddle contest.

"I'll write you a fiddle tune for your birthday," Daddy had said. "Tell me what kind you'd like."

The truth was I wanted a mountain bike for my birthday, but I knew my parents couldn't afford one, so I didn't even ask. I told him I wanted a tune that would get inside you without you realizing it—the kind of tune you'd find yourself humming when you walked along a country road on a star-filled night.

"Nina's Waltz" is just like that. It makes you close your eyes and sway. It takes you somewhere sweet. Daddy taught me "Nina's Waltz," and when I got the tune down well, he let me carry the melody alone. He fiddles variations all around it, and it is never the same piece twice. Sometimes he lets me play it on his fiddle.

By the time we got to the fiddle contest, the sun was up and the day had turned hot. I took off my sweatshirt, and I gave Daddy one of my ponytail clips to hold back his hair. People were stretched out on the grass all around a low wooden stage. There were fiddlers warming up everywhere—a woman in a long skirt with a wreath of flowers in her hair, a man whose plaid shirt barely buttoned across his fat belly, a kid in cowboy boots who didn't look a lot older than me. Daddy waved to a few fiddlers he knew.

Daddy loves to perform. But I'd never play in front of strangers. Just the thought of an audience makes my hands all sweaty and my stomach churn.

"As long as you enjoy playing for yourself, sweetie," Daddy always says, "that's all that matters."

I went up front with Daddy, where he registered for the contest. "N. Carey, number twenty-four," the man at the table said. Daddy looked at the names of the other contestants.

"There are some great fiddlers here today, Nina," he told me.

I squeezed Daddy's hand. "But no one as good as you," I said.

"Hope not," he said. "One thing I know for sure, though. 'Nina's Waltz' is a winner."

We spread our old quilt out on the grass and went back to the car for the fiddle and our lunch.

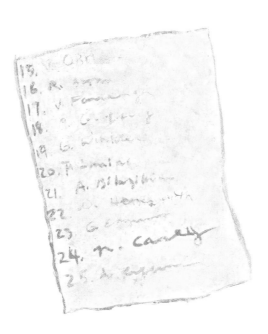

That's when it happened, and it happened so quickly I almost didn't see it. Some wasps had been out looking for lunch themselves and were sitting on the handle of Daddy's fiddle case. They stung him three times. Daddy's hand turned all red and swelled right up.

Daddy didn't cry, but I did. He looked like it hurt so much. He was given something to put on the stings and an ice pack. But there was no way he was going to be able to play the fiddle. He couldn't even bend his fingers.

"I guess we'll just have to wait for another time," said Daddy. "In the meantime we might as well stay and listen to the other fiddlers since we've come this far."

I couldn't say anything.

"Come on, sweetie, it's not the end of the world," said Daddy. "There will be other fiddle contests."

I knew that. Still, it felt like the end of the world to me. We'd gotten up so early to get to this contest, and we'd driven so far. Now Daddy wouldn't have a chance at the prize money, and Mom would be sorry that she hadn't made him stay home to work. And "Nina's Waltz" wouldn't be heard.

"Come, sit down now," Daddy said. "Let's enjoy the music as long as we're here."

I tried to do that. I lay back on our quilt and watched the sky while I listened to one fiddler after another. They were all good, but none of them were as good as Daddy. And there were a few good pieces, but none you'd find yourself humming, like "Nina's Waltz."

They were up to number seventeen. I looked at Daddy. He was watching the fiddler onstage. The ice pack was on his hand. His fiddle was behind him. He looked old and sad and tired.

He wasn't watching me at all. I opened his fiddle case. I took out his bow, tightened it, and rosined it carefully from frog to tip. I leaned down close and gently plucked the strings on the fiddle. They were pretty much in tune.

Daddy turned and looked back at me, a question on his face. But I'd already made up my mind. As number twenty-three walked up onstage, I made my way to the front and waited.

When the announcer called out "Number twenty-four," I stepped up to the table.

"N. Carey," he said, reading from his list. "Must be Nick Carey." Then he looked up and saw me.

"Well, miss," he said. "And who are you?"

"Nina Carey," I said.

"Nick's kid?"

I nodded.

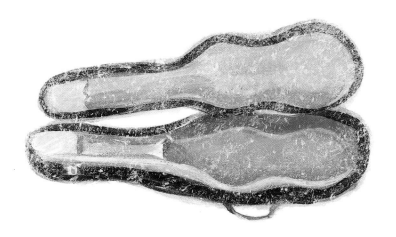

I walked up the three wooden steps to the stage. My hands were all sweaty and my stomach churned. I looked out at the lawn full of people. Some were lying back, watching the sky. Others were sitting up, like animals on their haunches.

I was all set to race off the stage, to run across that lawn of people, far across the green fields beyond them, toward the distant mountain. Then I spotted Daddy. He was watching me, waiting for me to play.

I thought of all the nights he had stayed up long after I had gone to sleep, working on "Nina's Waltz." I thought of the first time I'd heard him play it, right after I'd made my wish and blown out my birthday candles.

"Something for you to have your whole life long," he'd said.

I closed my eyes for a second, and then the tune was there. It was right there, in my head, in my fingers. And without even thinking, without even taking a breath, I tucked the fiddle under

my chin, lifted my bow, and let the tune out into that warm
sunshine, into that green afternoon.

I didn't win the fiddle contest, but I did get third place. Daddy insisted that the fifty dollars was all mine to spend. We looked through the want ads in the paper and found a used bike I could buy. It's red, with six speeds, and it looks almost new.

People ask me if I'll ever play onstage again and enter other contests, but I shake my head. The thought of playing for strangers still makes my hands all sweaty and my stomach churn. I did it, that once, for Daddy and for "Nina's Waltz." And for now, at least, that's good enough for me.